1,2,3 suddenly in EGYPT

The Eye of Horus

Cristina Falcón Maldonado

Illustrations: Marta Fàbrega

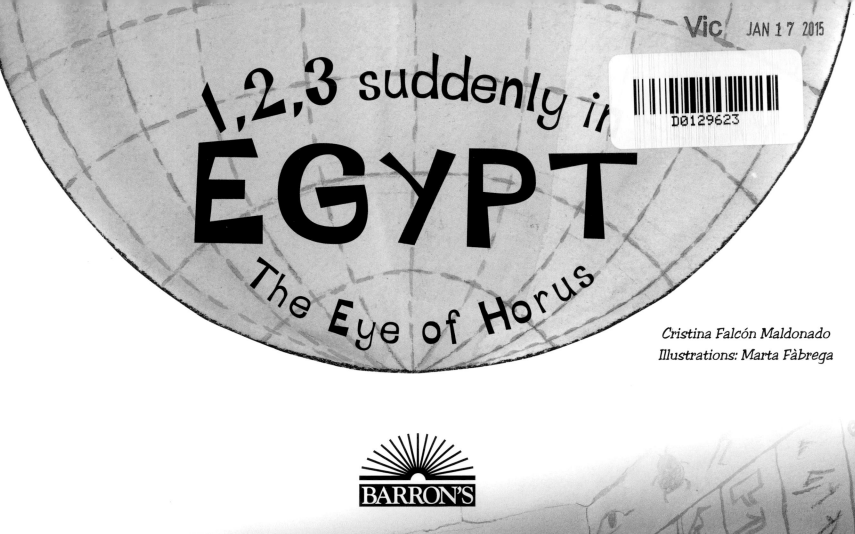

BARRON'S

On Martin's eighth birthday, his grandfather gave him a tiny package and said, "I've been an explorer all my life, and now it's your turn to see the world. Here is the key to my secret storeroom where you'll find everything you'll need."

In the secret storeroom, Martin found maps and equipment as well as his grandfather's travel album and a strange necklace that came with these instructions:

ATTACH STOREROOM KEY TO NECKLACE. PUT NECKLACE ON.

CLOSE EYES. NAME DESIRED DESTINATION OUT LOUD.

"Amazing! I can travel anywhere!" Martin said. So that very day, he went to China. He explored the country and brought back a small pet dragon. "What an adventure!" he thought. "Now, where in the world should I go next?"

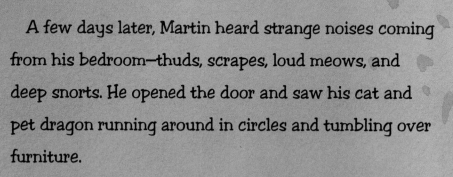

A few days later, Martin heard strange noises coming from his bedroom—thuds, scrapes, loud meows, and deep snorts. He opened the door and saw his cat and pet dragon running around in circles and tumbling over furniture.

"What's going on?" Martin shouted. The box containing his magic necklace was lying on the floor. As soon as he picked it up, he understood the cause of all the commotion. A large dark beetle was crawling on the lid of the box. "It looks just like my carved stone beetle," Martin thought, "the good luck charm that my grandfather brought back from Egypt." After staring at the live beetle for a minute, Martin exclaimed, "I get it! This is a message. It's time for my next adventure. It's time to explore Egypt!"

That night Martin packed for the trip. His hat, water bottle, first-aid kit, maps, stone beetle charm—everything went into his backpack. His pet dragon, whose name was See-me, watched the preparations, his ears twitching.

"You're as excited as I am," Martin said to See-me.

When he finished packing, Martin opened the travel album and read about his grandfather's trip to Egypt. He studied the drawings and photos. There was one photo of a man with gray hair and a gray moustache. Below it, Martin's grandfather had written: *My good friend, Khaled.*

"See-me," Martin said, "we must find Khaled. He'll help us explore Egypt."

Martin put on his backpack and slipped the magic necklace over his head. He held See-me in his arms, closed his eyes, and said . . . *"EGYPT!"* Then one, two, three, suddenly . . .

6-7

Martin was in Egypt. Not only that, he was in the middle of an Egyptian sand storm. When the air cleared, he realized he was standing in front of a man who looked like the photo of Khaled, but he was younger.

"Welcome, Martin!" the man said. "I am Tarek, the nephew of Khaled. My family and I have been waiting for you to arrive."

As he wiped the sand from his face, Martin thanked Tarek for his welcome and said, "I have no idea where we are."

Tarek laughed. "Turn around, and you'll know instantly."

Martin turned around and gasped. "There's the Great Sphinx! And the Great Pyramid!"

"Exactly right," Tarek said. "You're looking at the most famous monuments of ancient Egypt. The Great Sphinx is the largest statue in the world carved out of a single rock. It's also the oldest—4,500 years old."

Martin studied the sphinx. "It has a lion's body and a man's head."

Tarek nodded. "We think that the head represents King Khafre. One of the pyramids here is his tomb, and the sphinx was built to guard it."

8-9

"There are ten pyramids at Giza," Tarek said. "The biggest is the Great Pyramid, built for Pharaoh Khufu. The ancient Egyptians called their kings pharaohs. They believed a pharaoh's soul traveled to the heavens after death. The pyramid protected his body, which was preserved as a mummy. He was buried with household items, treasures, and even pets so he would have everything he needed in the afterlife."

Martin followed Tarek into the Great Pyramid where there were long passageways and several rooms.

"Look at all the hieroglyphs carved into the walls," Tarek said. "They're like small pictures, but they stand for words and sounds."

A few minutes later, Martin realized that he and See-me must have taken a wrong turn. They were completely alone in a passageway—and lost!

"How will we ever get out of here?" Martin asked nervously. He touched the lucky beetle charm that he wore around his neck. It seemed to glow like a flashlight. Suddenly, it flew through the air to an opening in the wall.

"Am I dreaming this?" Martin asked as he touched the wall.

"Yikes!" Martin shouted as he stumbled into a secret chamber. It was filled with cases of old papyrus scrolls. In his grandfather's album, Martin had read that the ancient Egyptians used the papyrus plant to make a paper-like material for writing. As Martin reached for one of the scrolls, he noticed that See-me was gone.

"See-me, come here!" he called. When the dragon didn't appear, Martin looked around the gloomy room. On one wall, a beam of light shaped like an eye marked the opening to a tunnel. Martin took a deep breath and started walking through the tunnel.

Martin walked until he reached the hot daylight outside the pyramid. He found See-me and Tarek waiting for him in the shade.

"There you are!" Martin and Tarek called out in the same instant. Tarek added, "Where did you get that papyrus scroll?"

Martin was puzzled. "I must have grabbed it when I left the secret chamber."

Tarek looked at the scroll. "Let's take this to the museum in Cairo," he said.

12-13

"Welcome to Cairo, Martin," Tarek said. "This is Egypt's capital city."

The streets were crowded with people, cars, carts, bicycles, and donkeys. Everyone seemed to be in a rush.

"You've arrived during Ramadan, our most important festival, " Tarek said. "We fast all day and then hurry home to eat a large meal at nightfall."

"Are all the lanterns part of the celebration?" Martin asked.

"Yes," Tarek said. "This kind of lantern is called a *fanous*. Most of them are made of tin and colored glass. Every child wants to carry one."

When they reached Tarek's home, his wife, Fatima, and his son, Ahmed, welcomed Martin with platters of food.

"Start with the *meze*—the appetizers," Ahmed said. "The eggplant *baba ghannoug* and lamb are my favorites. But save room for the *kushari*. It's one of our national dishes—rice, lentils, and chickpeas topped with spicy tomato sauce. And the desserts! Try the pancakes stuffed with apricots and—"

Fatima laughed. "Slow down, Ahmed. Martin hasn't been fasting like you."

14-15

The next day, Tarek took Ahmed and Martin to the Egyptian Museum. He left the boys to explore while he took the papyrus scroll to the museum's laboratory.

"There are more than one hundred thousand items from ancient Egypt here," Ahmed said. "Mummies, coffins—called sarcophagi—and even toys and games. But I'm going to show you the very best thing first."

"Wow! Double wow!" Martin said when they got to the display.

"This is the famous gold mask of Tutankhamun," Ahmed said. "He was only nine when he became pharaoh, and he died when he was eighteen. The mask covered the head and shoulders of his mummy in his tomb."

A cold shiver went up Martin's spine.
"I just saw the mask move!" he said.
"Let's get out of here," Ahmed said.
Then he saw something behind the mask,
something green. "It's your dragon,
Martin! See-me made the mask move!"
Martin sighed. "I should have named
him See-me-get-in-trouble."

16-17

Just before dawn, Martin woke up
to the sound of someone chanting.

"That's the call to prayer," Ahmed said. "Many
Egyptians pray five times a day."

After breakfast, Ahmed took Martin to Khan el-Khalili,
Cairo's oldest market.

"All these crisscrossing narrow streets," Martin said as they
wandered around. "It's like a maze, but a maze where you can
buy anything you can imagine."

When they got back to Ahmed's house, Tarek was packing the family van.

"I found out that the writing on the papyrus scroll is a magic spell," Tarek said. "But in order to find out more, we'll have to do some exploring. Be ready to leave on an adventure in five minutes!"

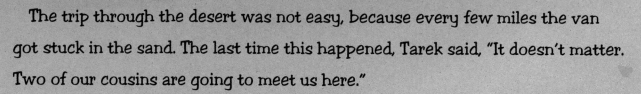

The trip through the desert was not easy, because every few miles the van got stuck in the sand. The last time this happened, Tarek said, "It doesn't matter. Two of our cousins are going to meet us here."

"There they are!" Ahmed shouted when a man and a boy rode up on a camel.

"Hello!" the man said as he jumped to the ground. "I'm Mohamed, and this is my son, Ayman. He's going to give Martin and Ahmed a ride to a fantastic place."

"A ride on a camel?" Martin asked. He was hoping the answer would be yes.

"Of course," Ahmed said. "Ayman is one of the best young camel riders in Egypt. He's been training for next week's big race."

Martin walked up to the camel. "Will this be like riding a horse?" he asked.

Ayman laughed. "If you like horseback riding, you'll love being on a camel."

20-21

Martin was enjoying the swooping, swaying motion of the camel ride when he noticed that the desert was turning green. They came to a place surrounded by palm trees.

"Is this a mirage?" Martin asked, "Something that looks real but isn't there at all?"

"No, this is very real," Ayman said. "It's an oasis—a place in the desert where there's a source of water. In fact, this is the Oasis of Siwa, one of the most beautiful oases of Egypt."

See-me dove into a pool of water even before the boys had climbed off the camel. Martin followed him. The water felt wonderfully cool after the dry heat of the desert. As the three boys swam around, Martin noticed some children who had climbed high up in the palm trees to gather dates.

"The Siwa dates are the sweetest in the desert," Ayman said. "Let's try some."

While the boys were snacking on dates, Tarek arrived in the van.

"I've got interesting news," he said. "A friend of mine in Siwa recognized the spell written on the papyrus scroll. It's a protection spell for someone on a journey."

"That's you!" Ayman said to Martin. "Now we know that you'll have a safe trip!"

22-23

The travelers drove to a narrow
rocky gorge called the Valley of the Kings.
"After building pyramids for tombs," Tarek said,
"the ancient Egyptians began burying their kings
here, in hidden tombs carved right into the rock."
"Guess how many tombs have been discovered
so far," Ahmed said. "More than sixty! But there
could be many more. I would love to discover one."

Tarek took the boys to see the tomb of Tutankhamun.

"Most tombs were robbed of their treasures long ago," Tarek said. "That's why this tomb is so important. When it was found, it still contained most of its treasures."

In the burial chamber, Martin and Ahmed stared at the pharaoh's sarcophagus.

"I just heard a strange noise," Martin said. "It sounded like a slithering snake."

"And I see it!" Ahmed whispered. "Let's get out of this place now!"

24-25

The next stop was a group of ancient temples at Karnac, just outside the city of Luxor. Martin couldn't believe his eyes when he stepped into the great hall of the temple dedicated to Amun-re, the sun god.

"This place must have been built for giants," he said, gazing up at columns that were almost seventy feet tall. "We could play a super game of hide-and-seek here."

"This temple was the largest in Egypt," Ahmed said, "and this room is the largest columned hall ever built anywhere in the world. It's perfect for hide-and-seek."

"How does anyone know what the hieroglyphs mean?" Martin wondered.

"We know thanks to a two-thousand-year-old slab of Egyptian stone called the Rosetta Stone," Tarek said. "A law had been carved into the stone in three different alphabets—hieroglyphs, Greek, and another version of Egyptian. By comparing the alphabets, experts figured out the meaning of the hieroglyphs."

"Get ready for a big surprise," Ahmed said as he and Martin stood on a dock on the Nile River. A minute later, a red and white sailboat glided up to the dock. Ahmed jumped aboard, shouting, "Follow me!"

Martin did just that. As soon as he saw who was sitting in the boat, he grinned. "You're Khaled, my grandfather's good friend! I recognize you from the photo."

"*Ahlan wa sahlan*, Martin," Khaled said. "Hello."

Martin was glad that Ahmed had taught him how to respond. "*Ahlan bik*," he said.

"We're about to repeat history," Khaled said. "On your grandfather's first trip to Egypt, I took him down the Nile in this same *felucca*. It's a traditional wooden sailing boat."

"Is it true that the Nile is the longest river in the world?" Martin asked.

Khaled nodded. "Absolutely. It's more than four thousand miles long. Along its banks, the desert blooms and the crops grow. For thousands of years, Egyptians have built their most important cities and monuments along the Nile."

28-29

Khaled sailed the boat to the city of Edfu so that Martin could visit the Temple of Horus, the best preserved temple in all Egypt.

"I really like the wall carvings and statues of Horus," Martin said. "He has a human body and the head of a falcon. Is there a story about him?"

"According to one ancient myth," Khaled said, "Seth, the evil god of the desert, killed his own brother Osiris, the pharaoh of Egypt, and took his throne. Then Osiris's son, Horus, overthrew Seth and became pharaoh and the powerful god of the Egyptians. It's a story about the victory of good over evil."

Pointing to a large carving of an eye, Martin said, "I've seen that before."

"It's the Eye of Horus," Ahmed said. "It provides protection and strength."

"That's how I found my way out of the Great Pyramid!" Martin said. "I saw a beam of light that looked just like the eye. It marked the opening of the tunnel."

"You're a very lucky traveler!" Khaled said. "You've been protected by your beetle charm, the spell on the papyrus scroll, and the Eye of Horus!"

Martin and his friends spent the next few days sailing south on the Nile River.

"We have a long way to go," Ahmed said, "so I'll teach you how to play the favorite game of the pharaohs. It's a board game called *senet*."

Many games later, they reached the two Temples of Abu Simbel.

"The pharaoh Ramses II had these temples carved out of the mountainside next to the Nile," Khaled explained. "Gigantic statues of him guard the entrances."

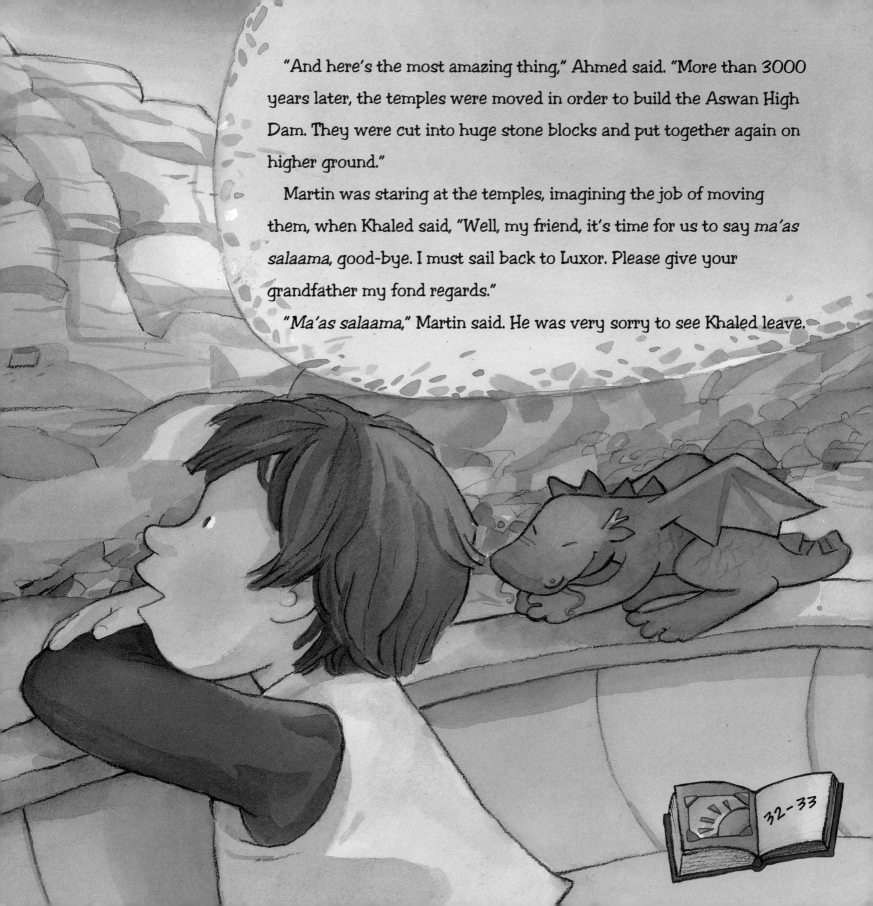

"And here's the most amazing thing," Ahmed said. "More than 3000 years later, the temples were moved in order to build the Aswan High Dam. They were cut into huge stone blocks and put together again on higher ground."

Martin was staring at the temples, imagining the job of moving them, when Khaled said, "Well, my friend, it's time for us to say *ma'as salaama*, good-bye. I must sail back to Luxor. Please give your grandfather my fond regards."

"*Ma'as salaama*," Martin said. He was very sorry to see Khaled leave.

32-33

Just before Tarek and Ahmed returned to Cairo, they took Martin snorkeling in the Red Sea, on Egypt's east coast.

Ahmed told him that it was called the Red Sea because the algae on the surface of the water make it look red in the summer.

"Let's jump in!" Martin shouted.

The boys swam along the coral reefs, gazing at dozens of different kinds of fish. Martin knew that some of them existed nowhere else in the world.

"Egypt is awesome," he thought. "You can go from ancient temples in the desert to an underwater world like this. You can—Hey!" Martin felt his beetle charm slip off his neck. He lunged forward and managed to grab it just as Ahmed signaled that it was time to go back to shore.

Martin said *ma'as salaama* to Tarek and Ahmed and watched their van disappear down the road. Then he put on his magic necklace and held See-me in his arms. He took one long last look at the Red Sea, closed his eyes, and said, *"HOME!"*

34-35

1,2,3 suddenly in
EGYPT
The Eye of Horus

GLOSSARY

MUMMY: Egyptians wanted to preserve the bodies of dead people. The body was treated with chemicals, wrapped with linen strips, and kept in a coffin called *sarcophagus*. (Page 10)

FANOUS: Metal lanterns with colored glass, used especially during Ramadan. They are traditionally given to children, who enjoy playing with them at that time of year. (Page 15)

MEZE: Assorted cold appetizers, typical of Egypt, served with Arabic bread called *aish balladi*. (Page 15)

BABA GHANNOUG: Eggplant puree with sesame seed paste and spices. (Page 15)

KUSHARI: A very popular and typical Egyptian dish made from rice, lentils, chickpeas, pasta, and tomato sauce. (Page 15)

AHLAN BIK: Reply to the welcome greeting given to a man. (Page 29)

FELUCCA: Traditional Egyptian boat, built of wood, with one or two sails. (Page 29)

First edition for the United States and Canada published in 2011 by Barron's Educational Series, Inc.
© Copyright 2010 by Gemser Publications, S.L.
C/Castell, 38; Teià (08329) Barcelona, Spain (World Rights)
Author: Cristina Falcón Maldonado
Adaptation of English Text: Joanne Barkan
Illustrator: Marta Fàbrega

Revision and iconography: Enriqueta de Francisco. Master in Egyptology; from the Fundació Arqueològica Clos of the Egyptian Museum, Barcelona

All inquiries should be addressed to:
Barron's Educational Series, Inc.
250 Wireless Boulevard
Hauppauge, NY 11788
www.barronseduc.com

ISBN-13: 978-0-7641-4584-1
ISBN-10: 0-7641-4584-3

Library of Congress Control No.: 2010931207

Date of Manufacture: December 2010
Manufactured by: L. Rex Printing, Tin Wan, Aberdeen, Hong Kong

Printed in China
9 8 7 6 5 4 3 2 1